This
Iggy Pig

book belongs to:

• •

Iggy Pig's Party

Written by

Vivian French

Illustrated by

David Melling

*Hodder
Children's
Books*

A division of Hodder Headline Limited

For Joe
With much love
Vivie

For Liberty Bennett
D. M.

It was Iggy Pig's birthday.

"Mother Pig, Mother Pig!"
said Iggy Pig. "Can I have a
party at four o'clock today?"

1

"Oink," said Mother Pig.

"You are my own dear Iggy Pig.

Of course you may have a party."

"HURRAH!" said Iggy Pig.

"HURRAH!"

He went dancing around
the farmyard.
"I'm going to have a party!
I'm going to have a party!
I'm going to have a party
at four o'clock today!"

Behind the hedge was a big grey
animal. A big grey animal with
a long bushy tail.

"AHA!" said the big grey animal.
"AHA!" and he smiled a hungry
smile.

Tabby Cat heard Iggy Pig
singing.

"Miaow! Miaow!" said Tabby
Cat.

"Are you going to invite me
to your party, Iggy Pig?"

"Oh YES, Tabby Cat," said Iggy
Pig. "Of course you can come to
my party!"

"Miaow! Miaow!" said Tabby
Cat. "I hope you will have
a slippery fish for me to eat!"

"Oh YES, Tabby Cat," said Iggy Pig. "There will be a BIG slippery fish."

"Good," said Tabby Cat. "Then I'll come."

Iggy Pig went dancing around
the farmyard.
"I'm going to have a party!
I'm going to have a party!
I'm going to have a party
at four o'clock today!"

Behind the wall was the big
grey animal.

The big grey animal with
the long bushy tail.

The big grey animal with
the hungry smile.

"AHA!" said the big grey animal,
and his tummy rumbled.

Dusty Dog heard Iggy Pig
singing.

"Woof! Woof!" said Dusty Dog.
"Are you going to invite me to
your party, Iggy Pig?"

"Oh YES, Dusty Dog," said Iggy
Pig. "Of course you can come to
my party!"

"Woof! Woof!" said Dusty Dog.
"I hope there will be a big juicy
bone for me to eat!"

"Oh YES, Dusty Dog," said Iggy
Pig. "There will be a HUGE juicy
bone."

"Good," said Dusty Dog.
"Then I'll come!"

Iggy Pig went dancing around
the farmyard.

"I'm going to have a party!
I'm going to have a party!
I'm going to have a party
at four o'clock today!"

Behind the fence was the big
grey animal.

The big grey animal with
the long bushy tail.

The big grey animal with
the hungry smile.

14

The big grey animal with
the rumbling tummy.

"AHA!" said the big grey animal,
and he licked his lips.

Iggy Pig danced all the way
home.

"I'm going to have a party!
I'm going to have a party!
I'm going to have a party
at four o'clock today!"

"That's right, my own dear Iggy
Pig," said Mother Pig.
"We will have cabbage leaves
to crunch.
We will have potato peelings
to munch.
We will sing Happy Birthday
to you!"

"Mother Pig, Mother Pig!"
said Iggy Pig. "We must have a
BIG slippery fish for Tabby Cat!"

Mother Pig shook her head.

"Dear me, Iggy Pig. Where would
we find a slippery fish? Cabbage
leaves are MUCH nicer!"

"We must have a HUGE juicy
bone for Dusty Dog!"

Mother Pig shook her head.

"Dear me, Iggy Pig. Where would
we find a juicy bone? Potato
peelings are MUCH better!"

Iggy Pig went sadly outside.

"I need a BIG slippery fish.

I need a HUGE juicy bone.

I don't want to eat cabbage

leaves all by myself.

I don't want to eat potato

peelings all by myself."

The big grey animal stepped
out from behind a tree.
"AHEM!" he said.

"WHO ARE YOU?" asked
Iggy Pig.

"Just a friend," said the big grey
animal. "Dear little pig – did you
say you wanted a slippery fish?"
"That's right," said Iggy Pig.

"And, dear little pig – you
wanted a big juicy bone?"
"Yes please!" said Iggy Pig.

"EASY!" said the big grey
animal.

"I'll fetch them straight away.
Oh – little pig! You will invite
ME to your party, won't you?"

"OF COURSE I will!"
said Iggy Pig.

Iggy Pig went dancing
around the farmyard.
"I'm going to have a party!
I'm going to have a party!
I'm going to have a party
at four o'clock today!"

It was five minutes before
four o'clock.

The big grey animal came
up to Iggy Pig.
"Here you are little pig!
Here is the slippery fish!
Here is the juicy bone!
Eat them up quickly!
Eat them up quickly
and get FAT!"

"Oh NO!" said Iggy Pig.

"I don't like slippery fish.

I don't like juicy bones.

I like cabbage leaves

and potato peelings.

What do YOU like

big grey animal?"

30

The big grey animal licked
his lips.

The big grey animal's tummy
rumbled.

The big grey animal smiled
his hungry smile.

"I like – LITTLE PIGS!"

he said, and he JUMPED...

JUST as Dusty Dog and Tabby
Cat came around the corner.

"WOOF! WOOF! WOOF!"

barked Dusty Dog.

He showed his sharp white teeth.

"MIAOW! MIAOW!" miaowed
Tabby Cat. She showed her sharp
shiny claws.

"WOWLY! WOWLY!" howled
the big grey animal.

He turned right round
and he ran...

He ran and he ran and he ran...

"Four o'clock!" said Iggy Pig.

"Time for my party!"

37

Tabby Cat ate her
BIG slippery fish.
Dusty Dog crunched his
HUGE juicy bone.

Iggy Pig crunched cabbage
leaves, and munched potato
peelings until he was all
filled up...
And they all sang:

Happy Birthday to you!

Iggy Pig went to bed that night
feeling very full and happy.
"That was the best party ever!"
he said.

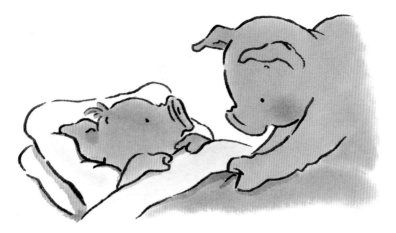

"Indeed it was, my own dear
Iggy Pig," said Mother Pig.
"It was so clever of you to find a
slippery fish AND a juicy bone."

"Oh," said Iggy Pig.

"I didn't find them.

The big grey animal did."

And he yawned a great big yawn.

"OINK!" said Mother Pig.

"OINK! OINK! OINK!

Iggy Pig! Iggy Pig! Have you

been talking to a WOLF?"

Iggy Pig didn't answer.

Iggy Pig was fast asleep.